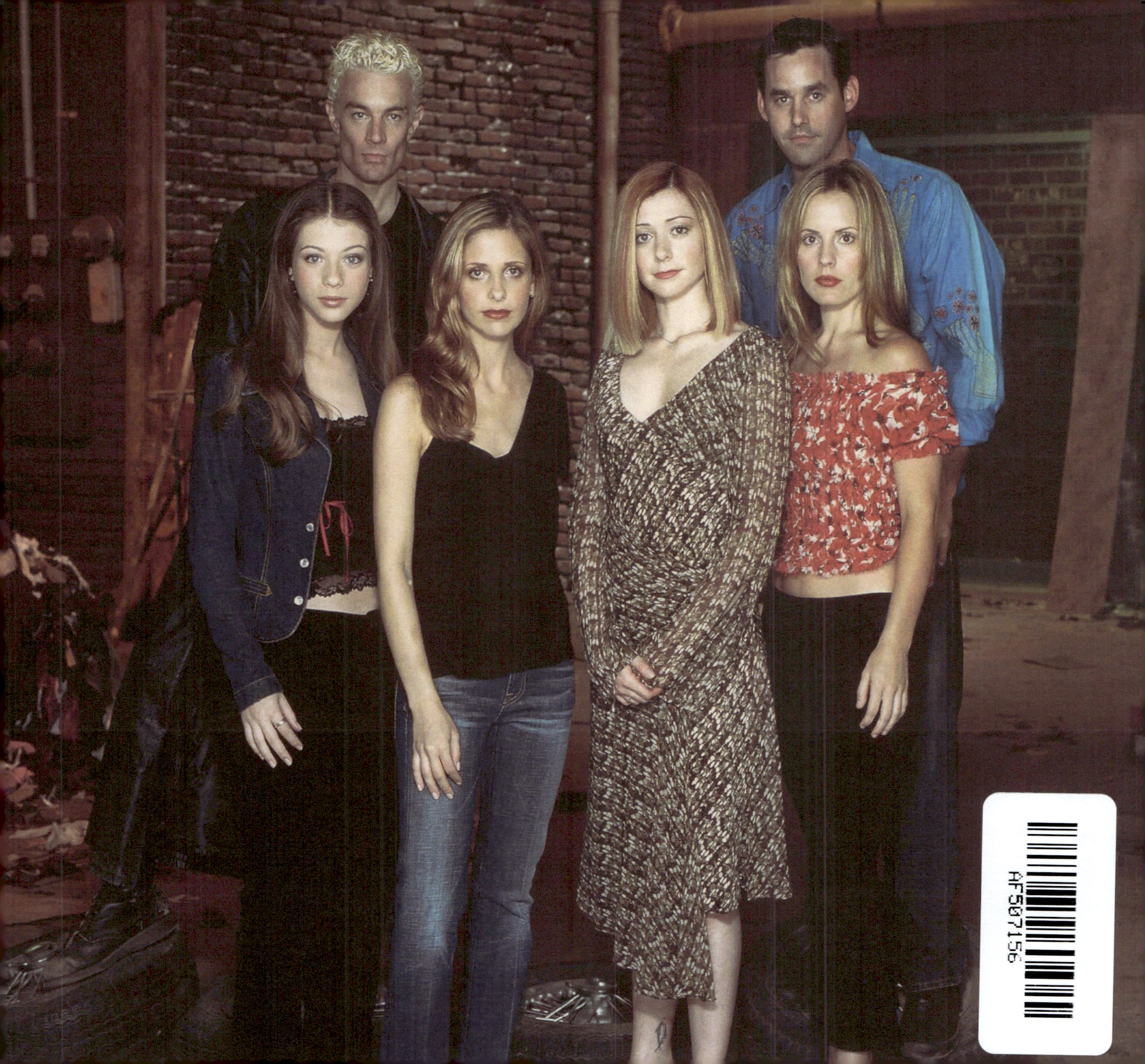

AF507156

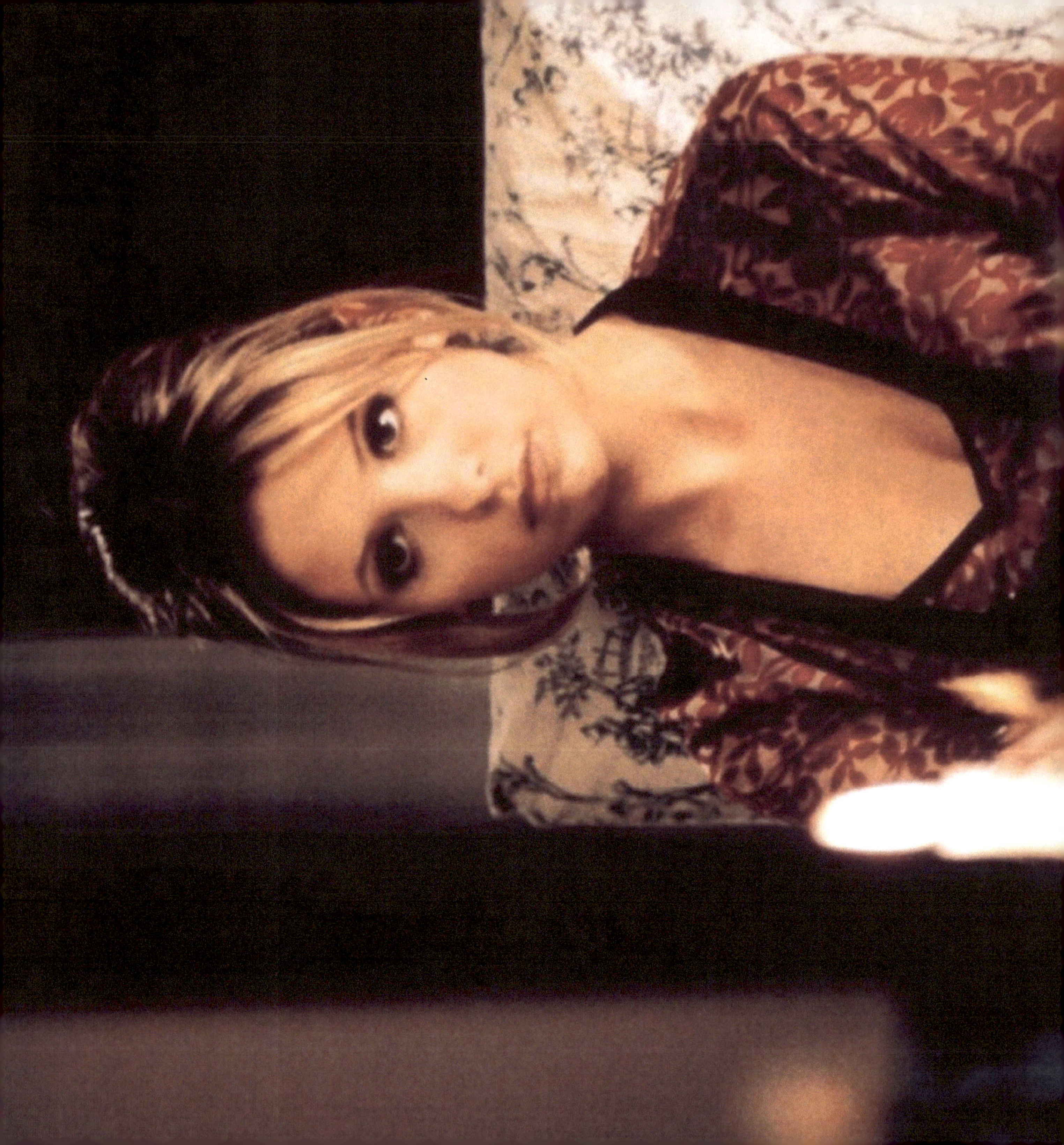

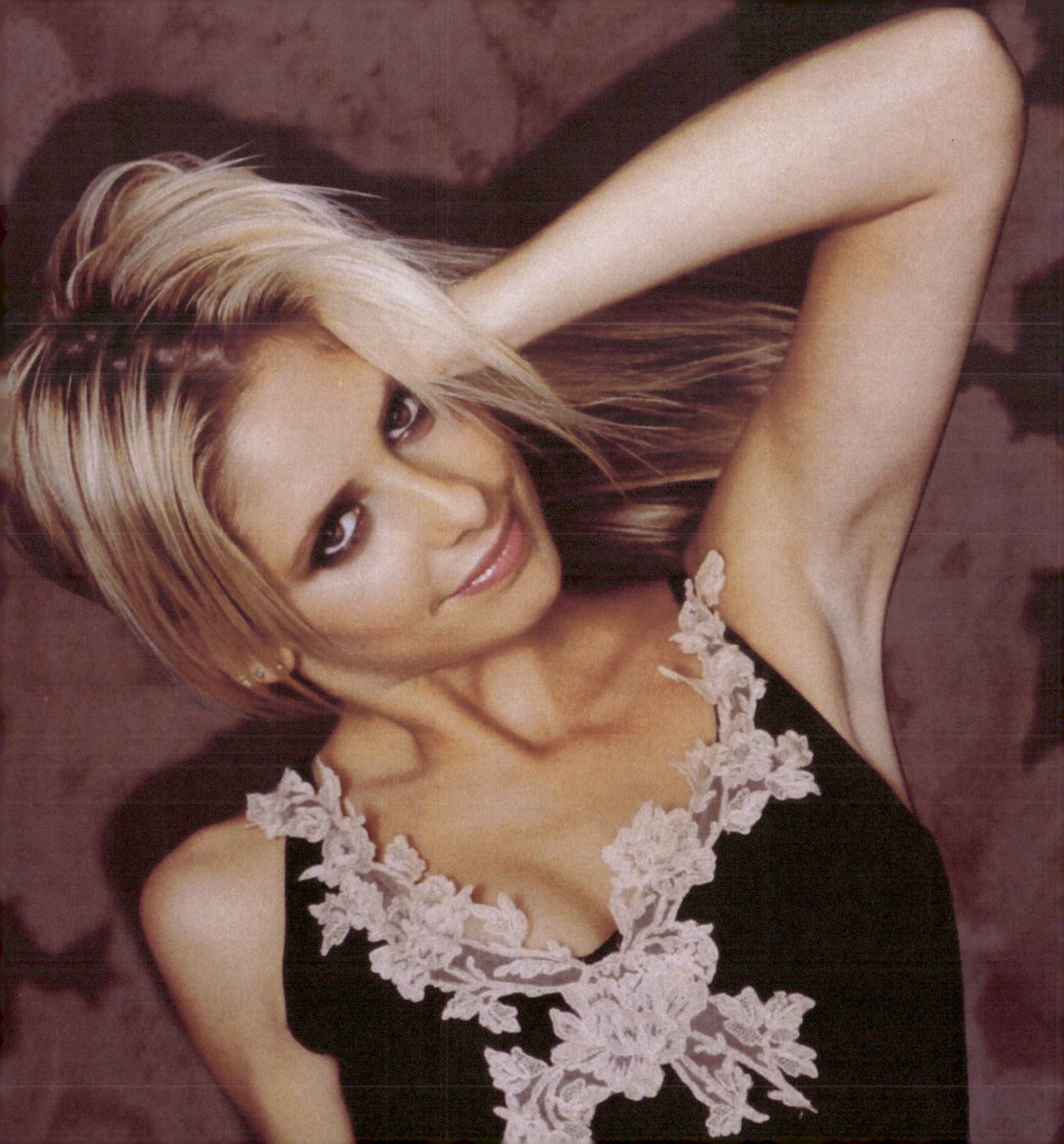

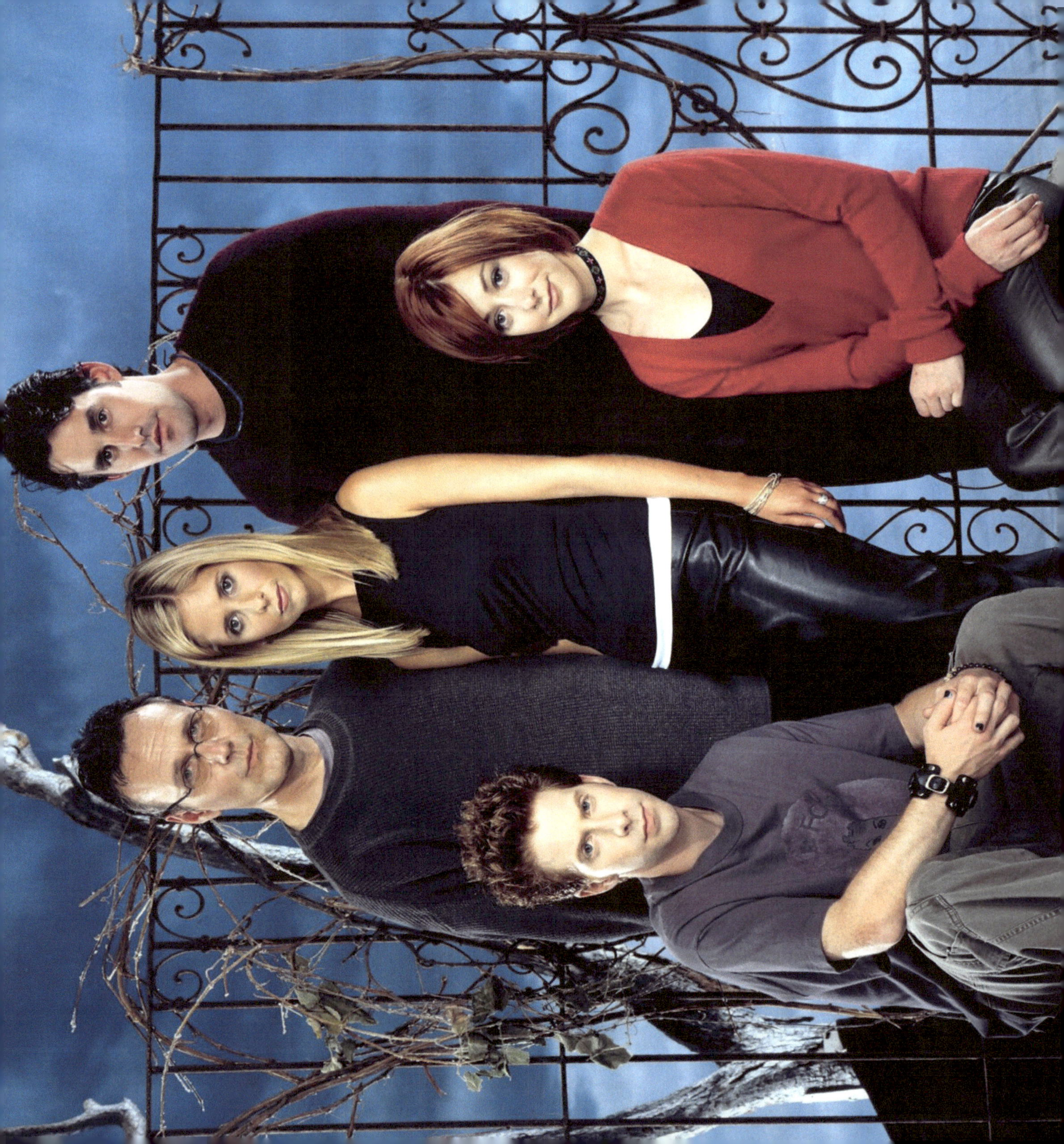

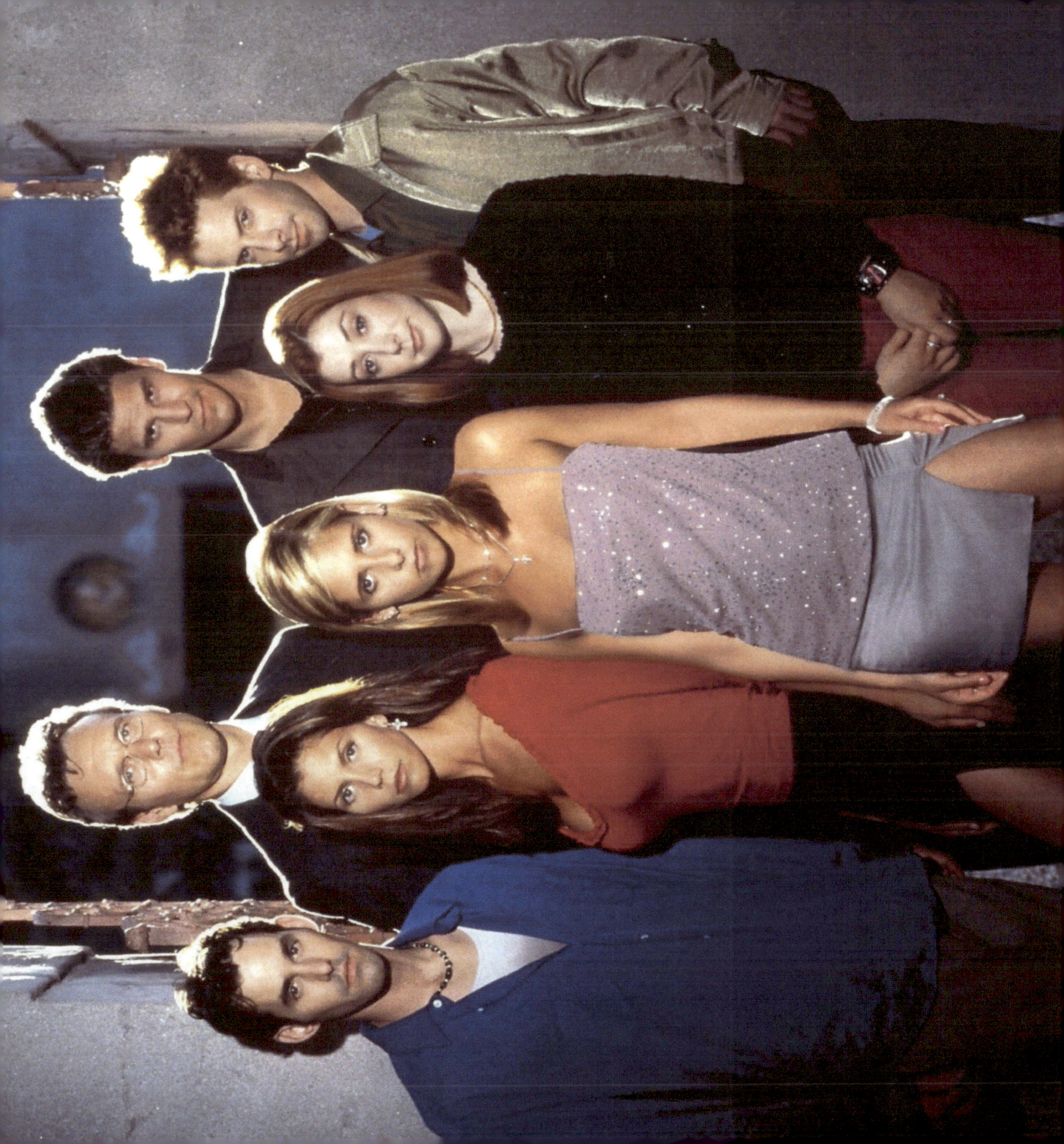

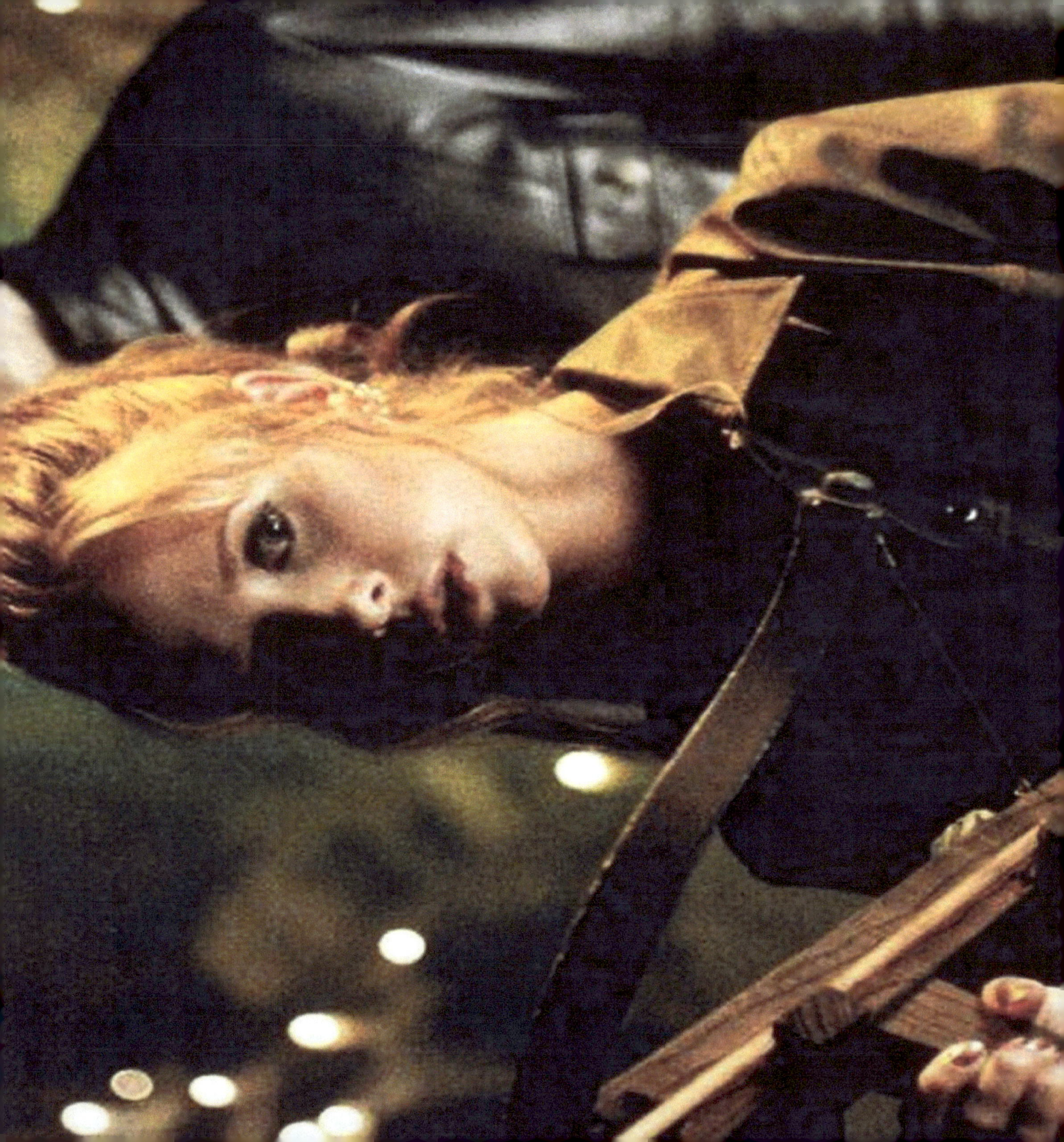

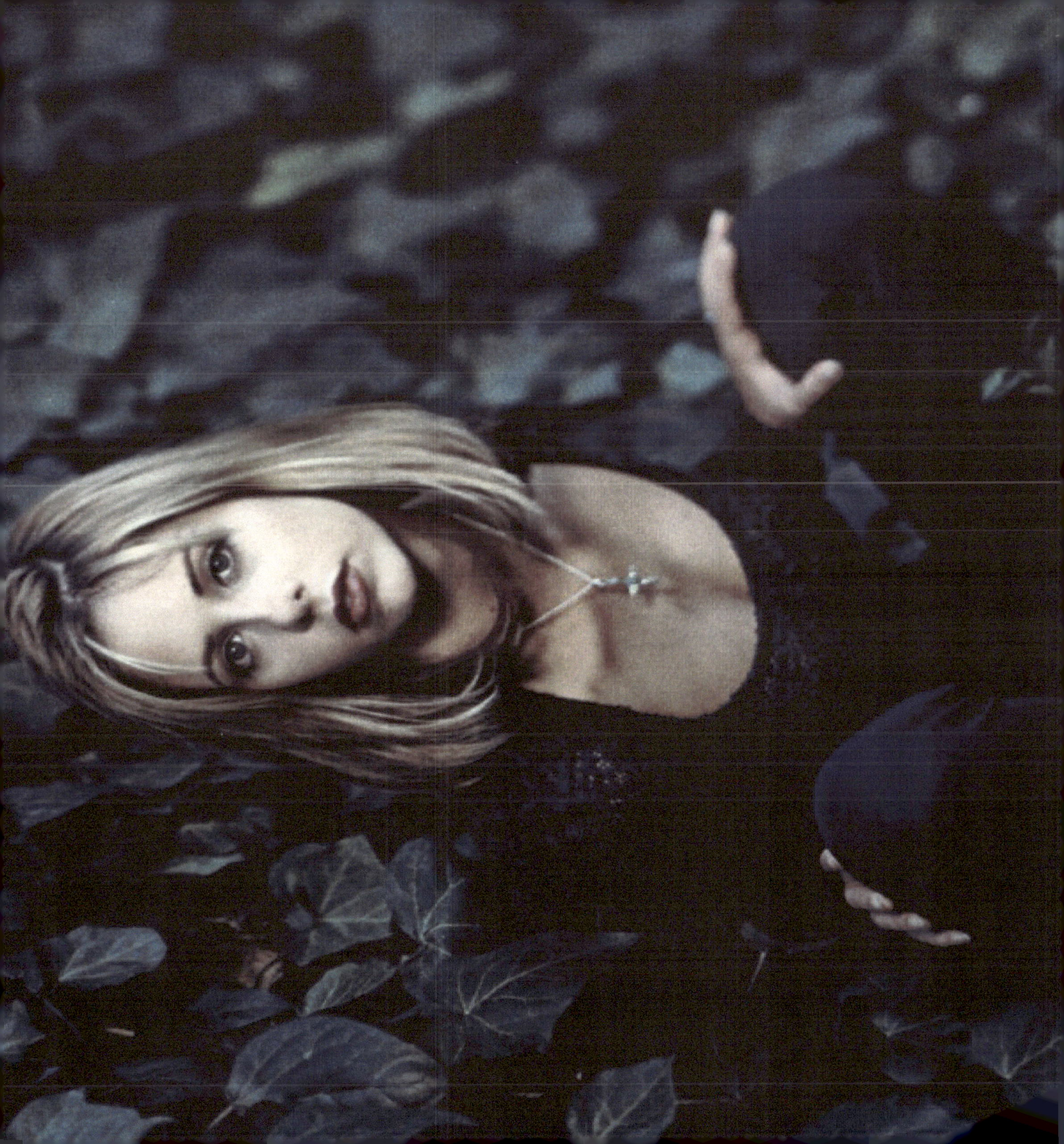

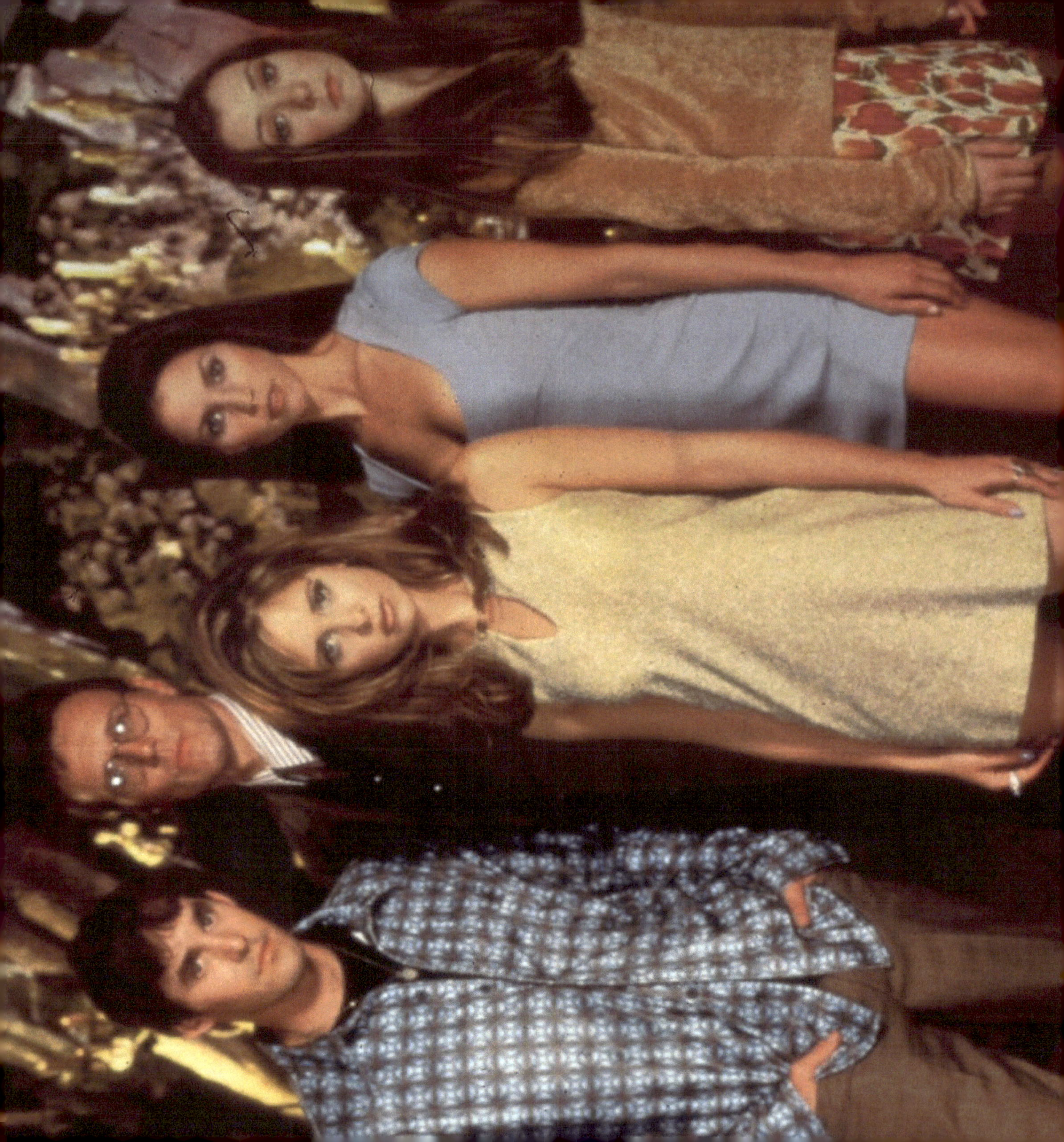

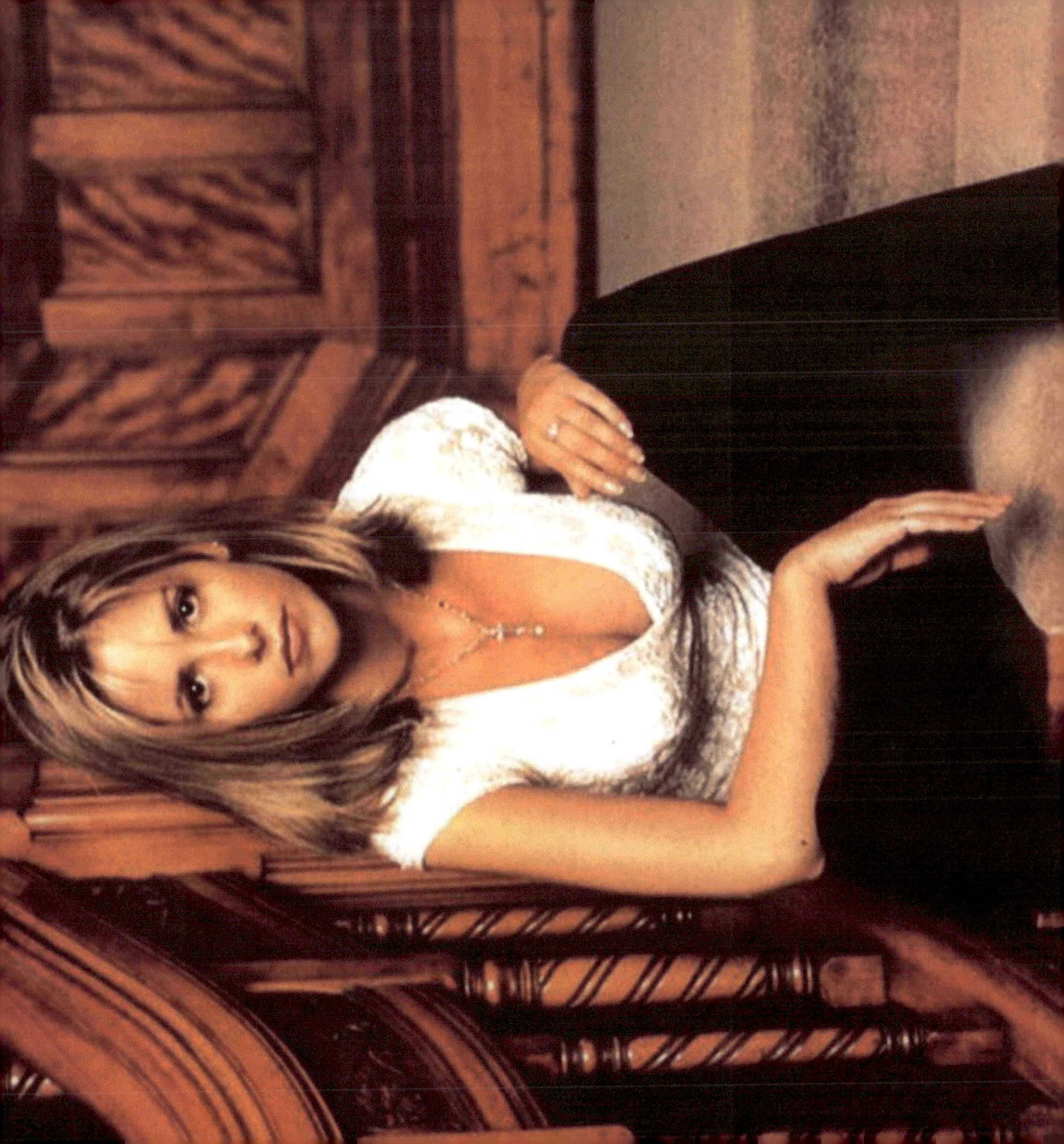

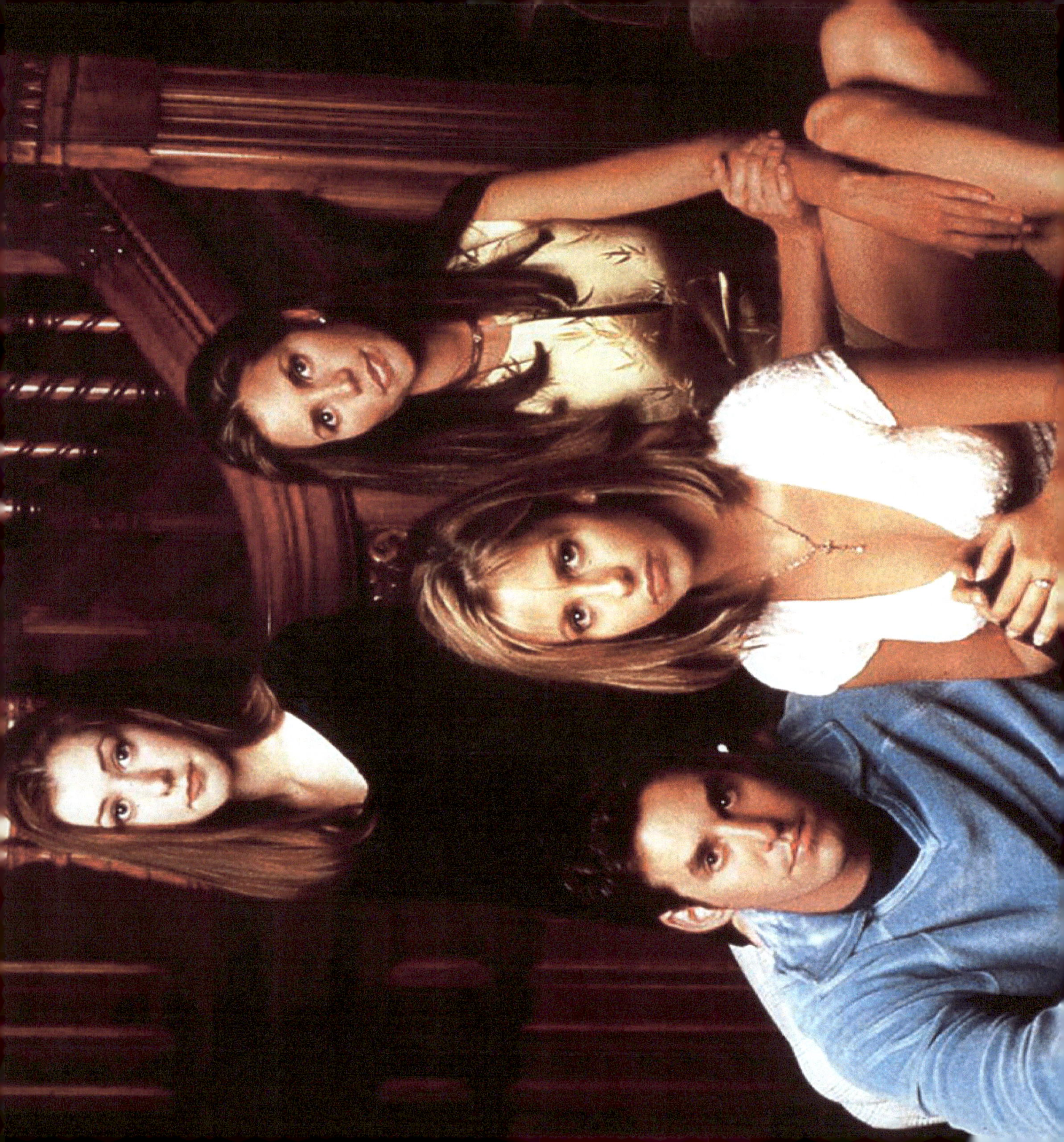

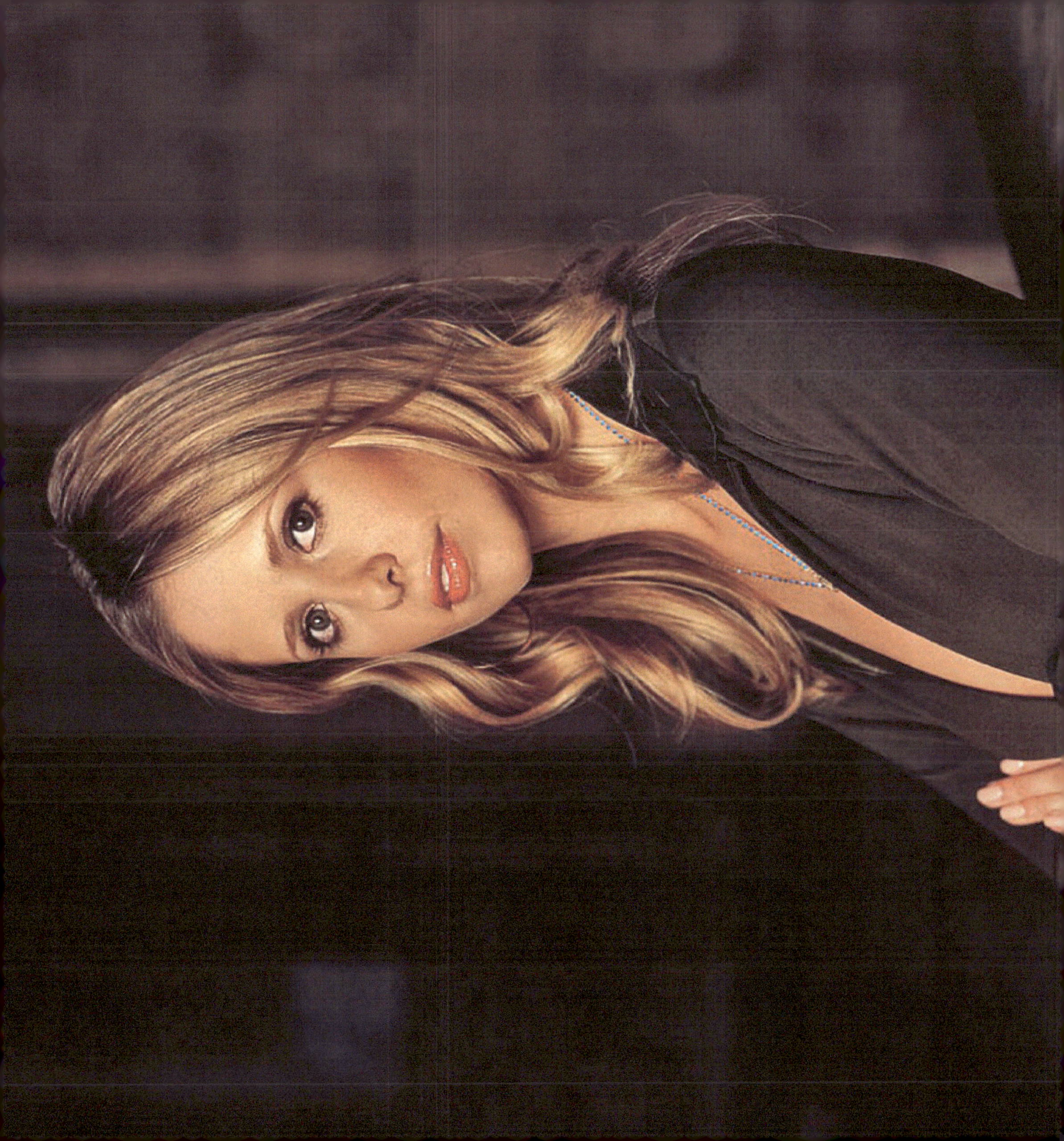

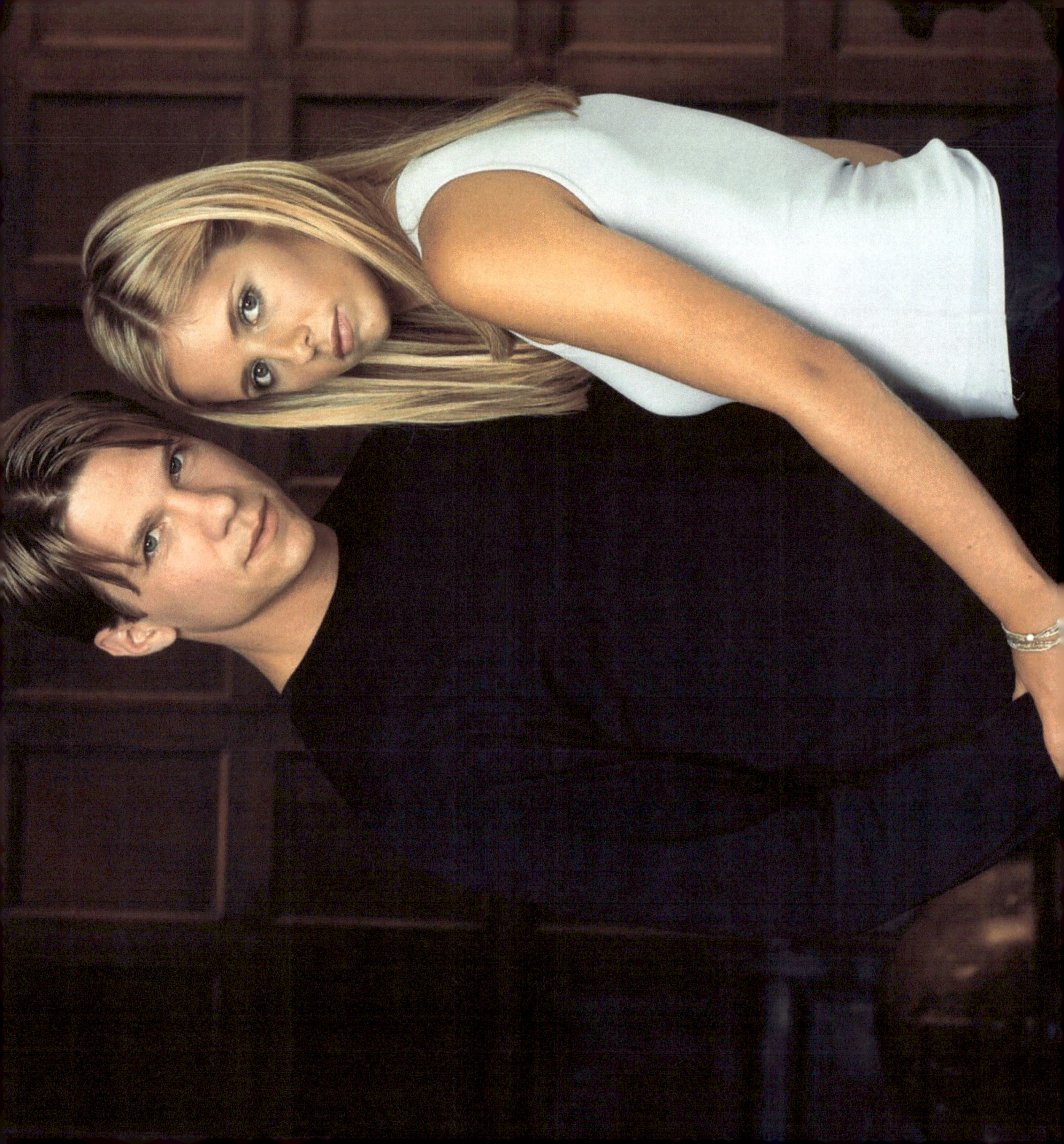

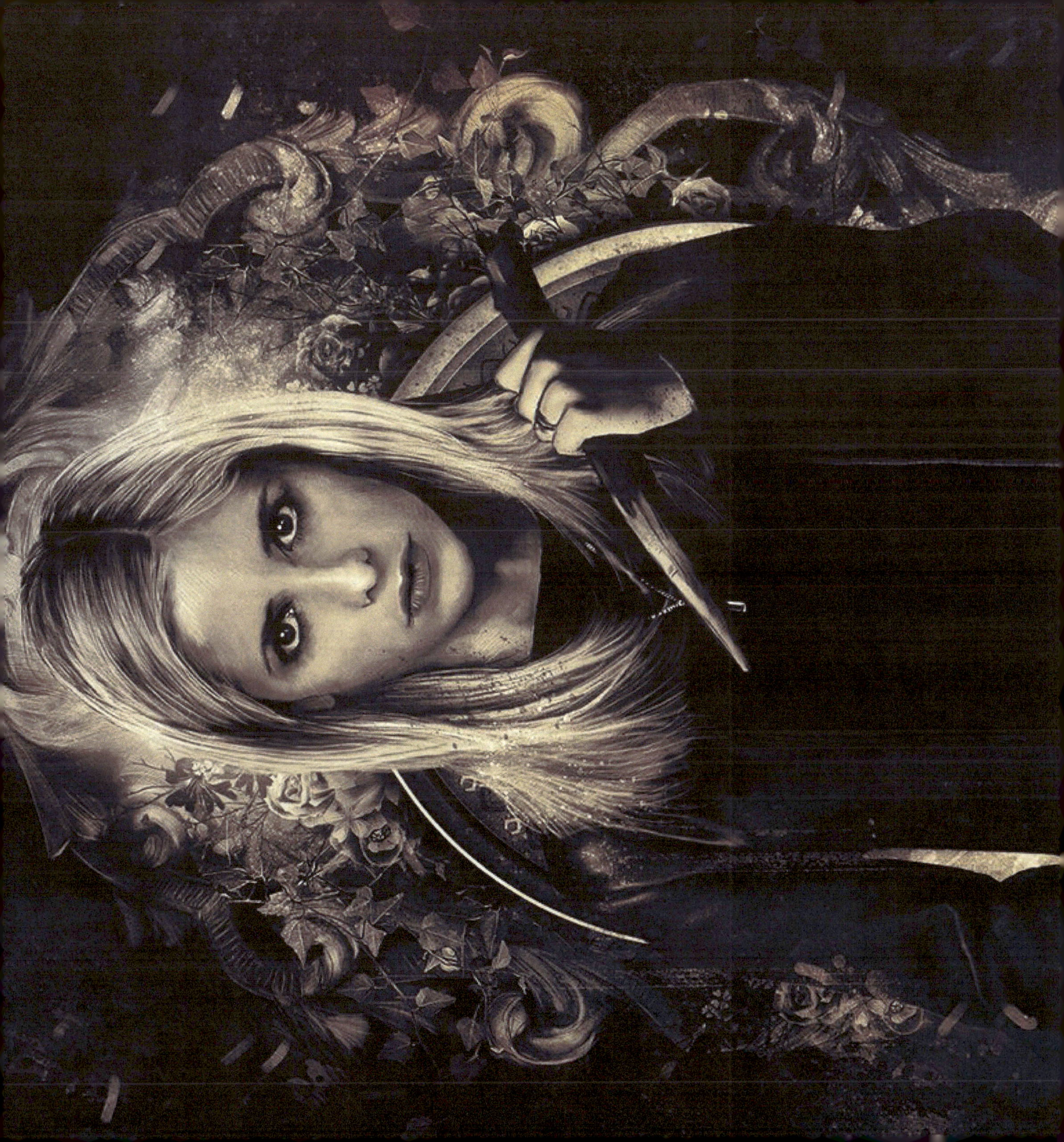

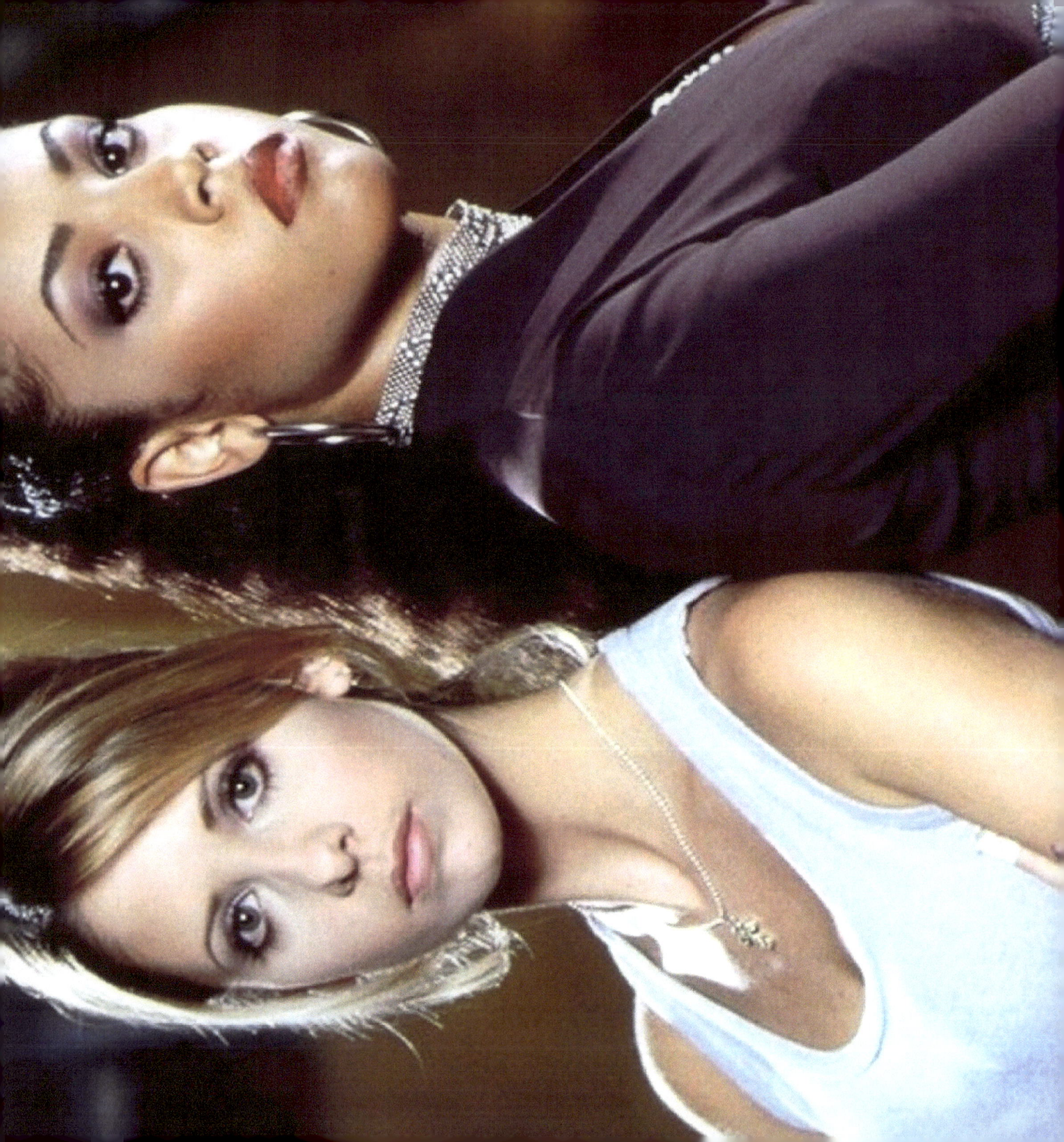

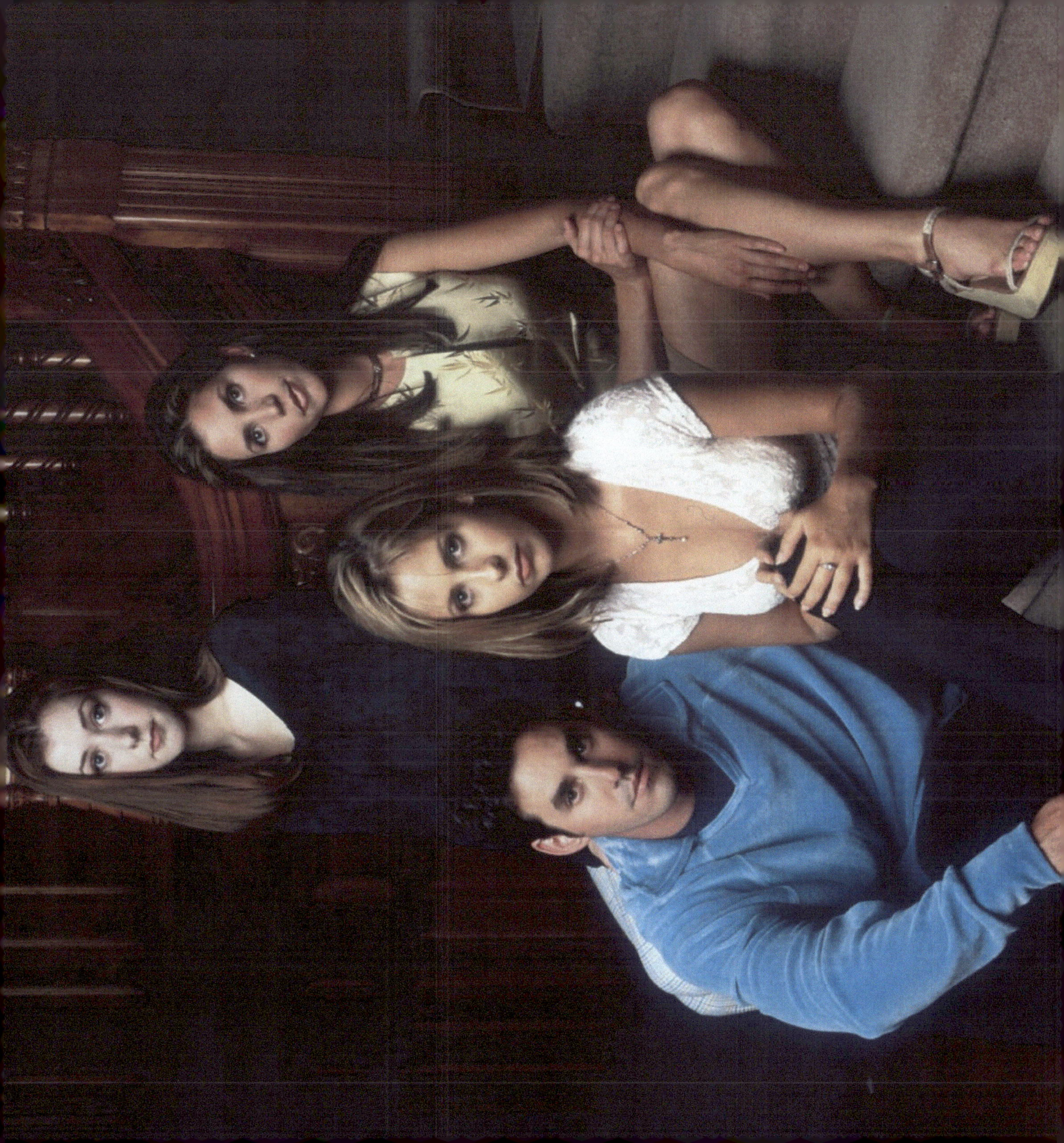

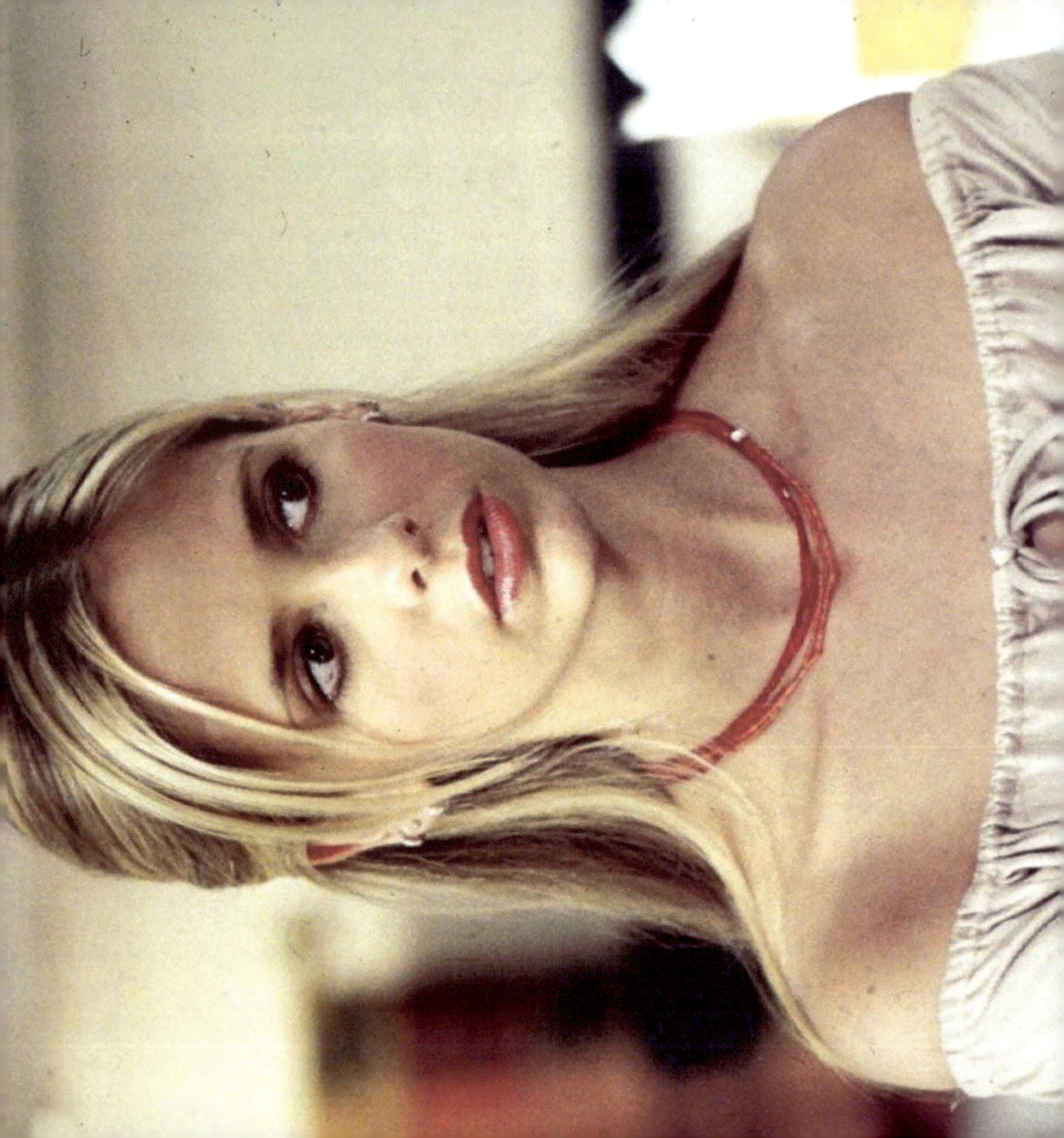

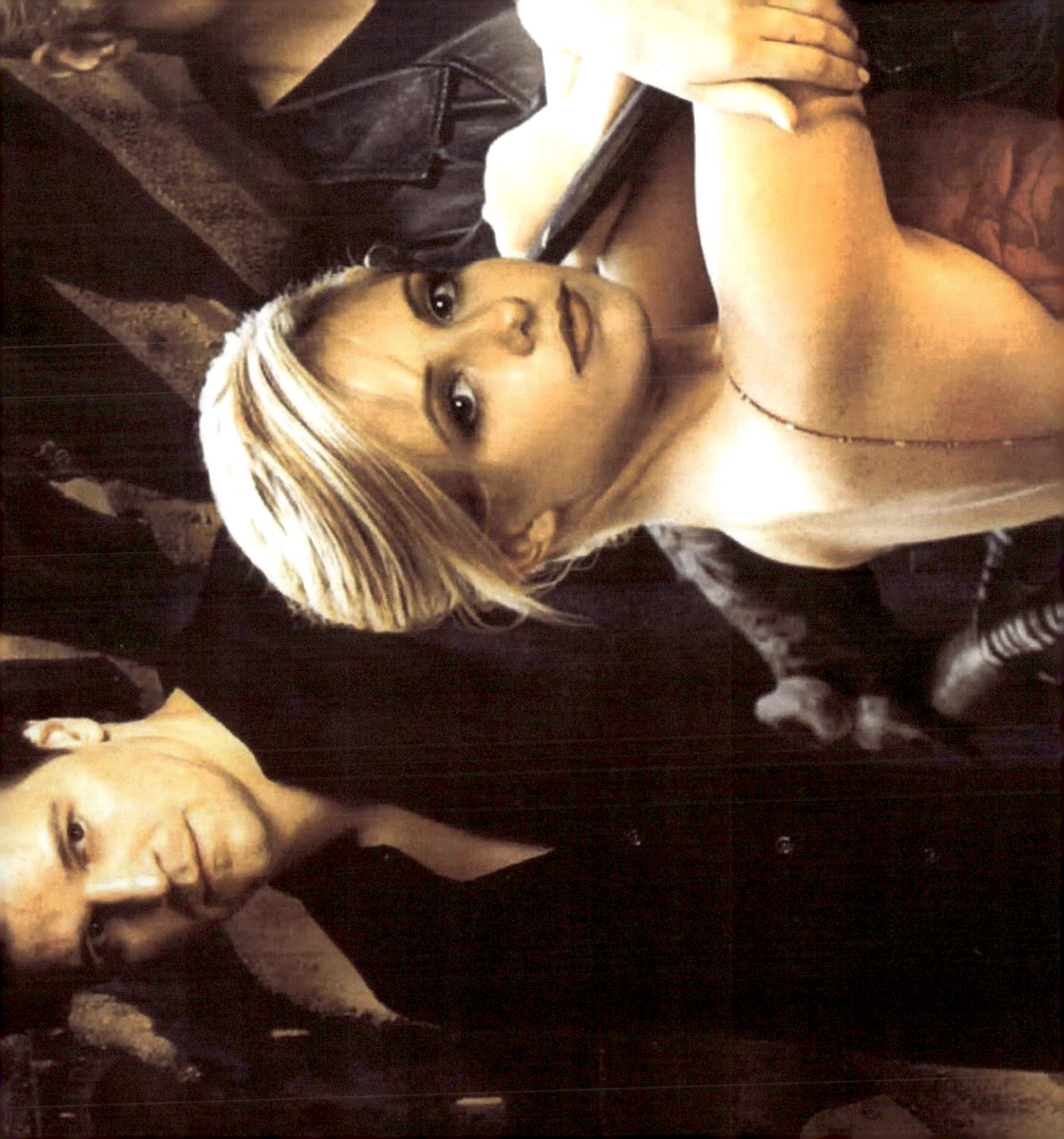

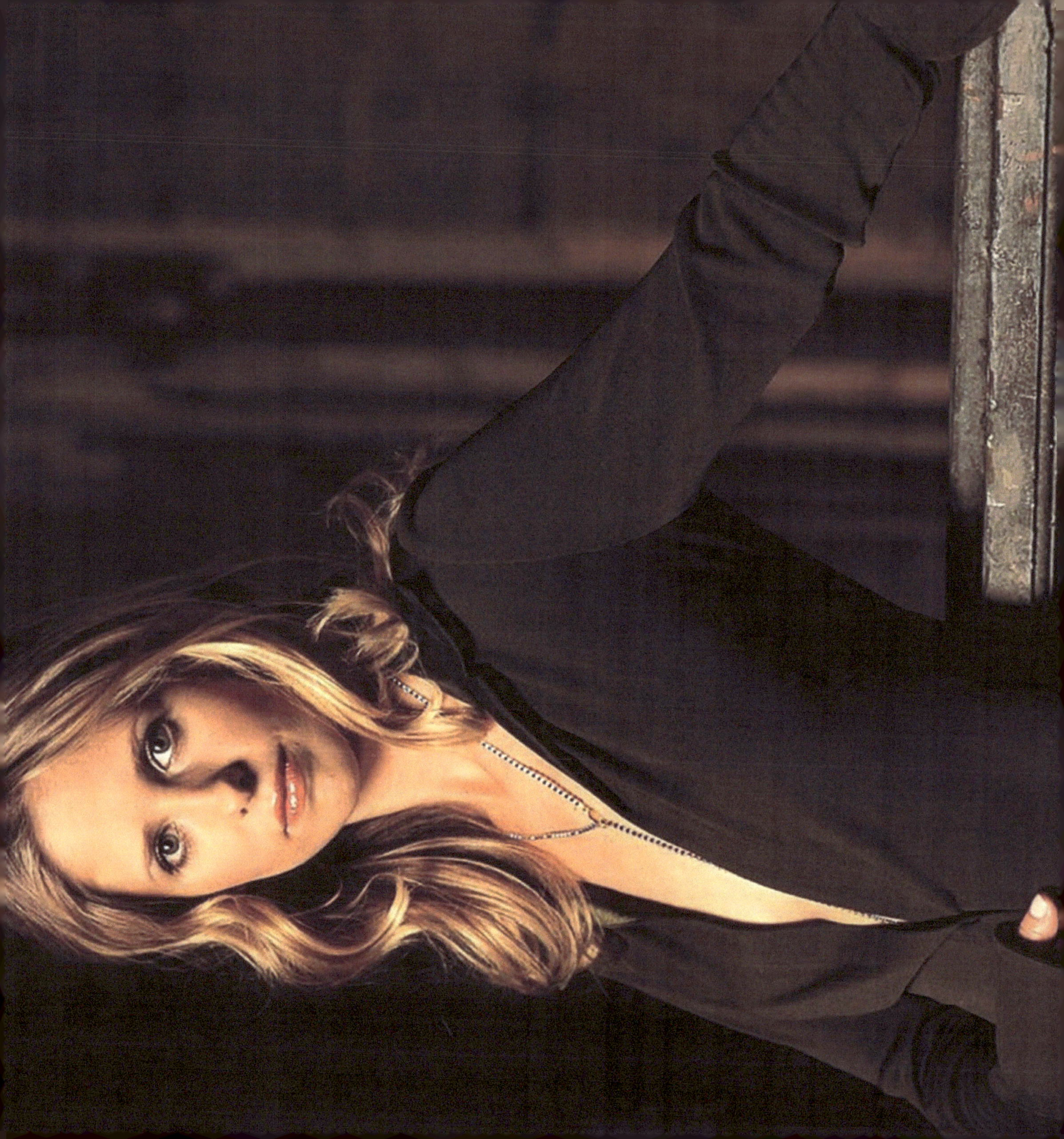

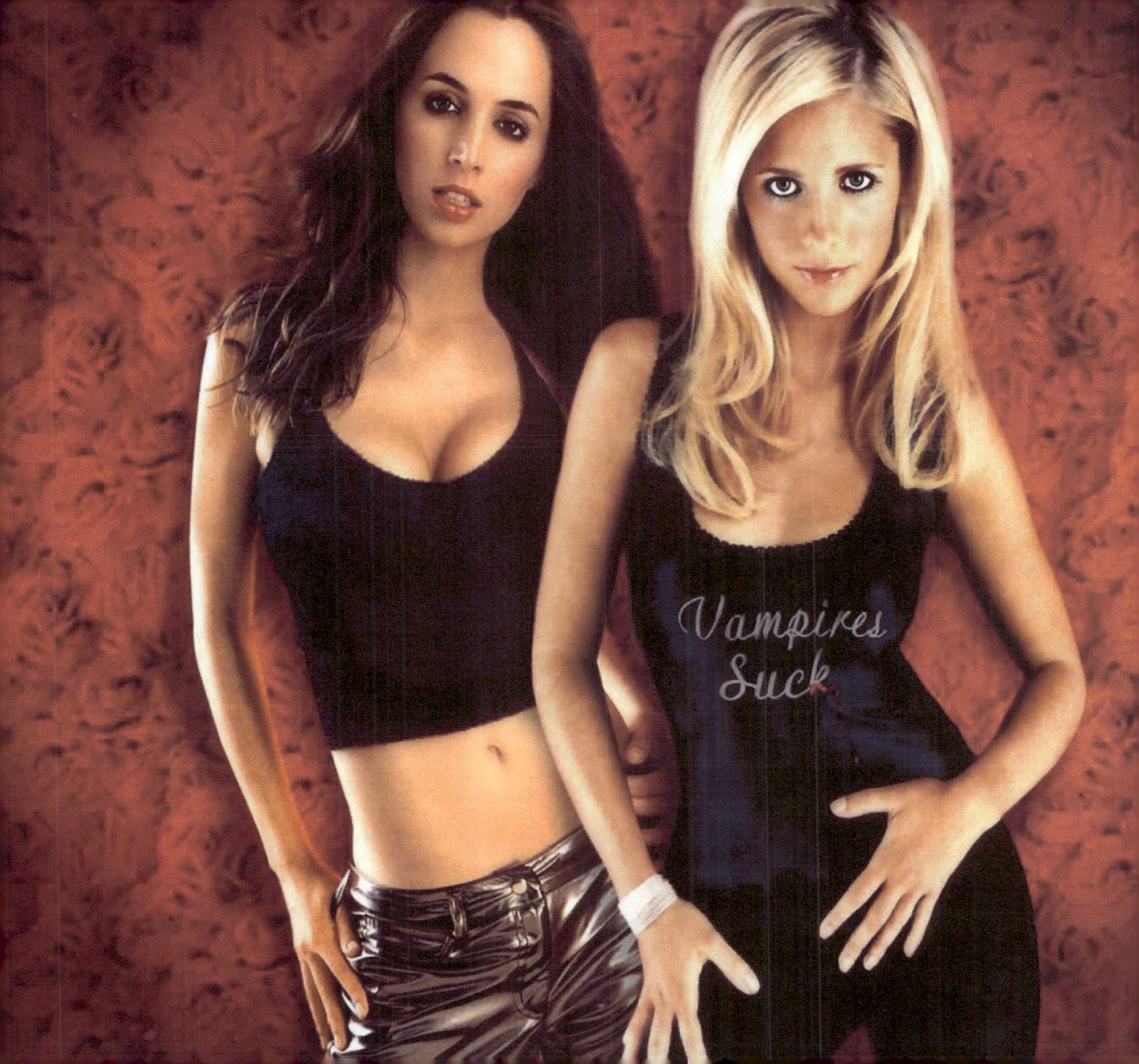
Vampires
Suck

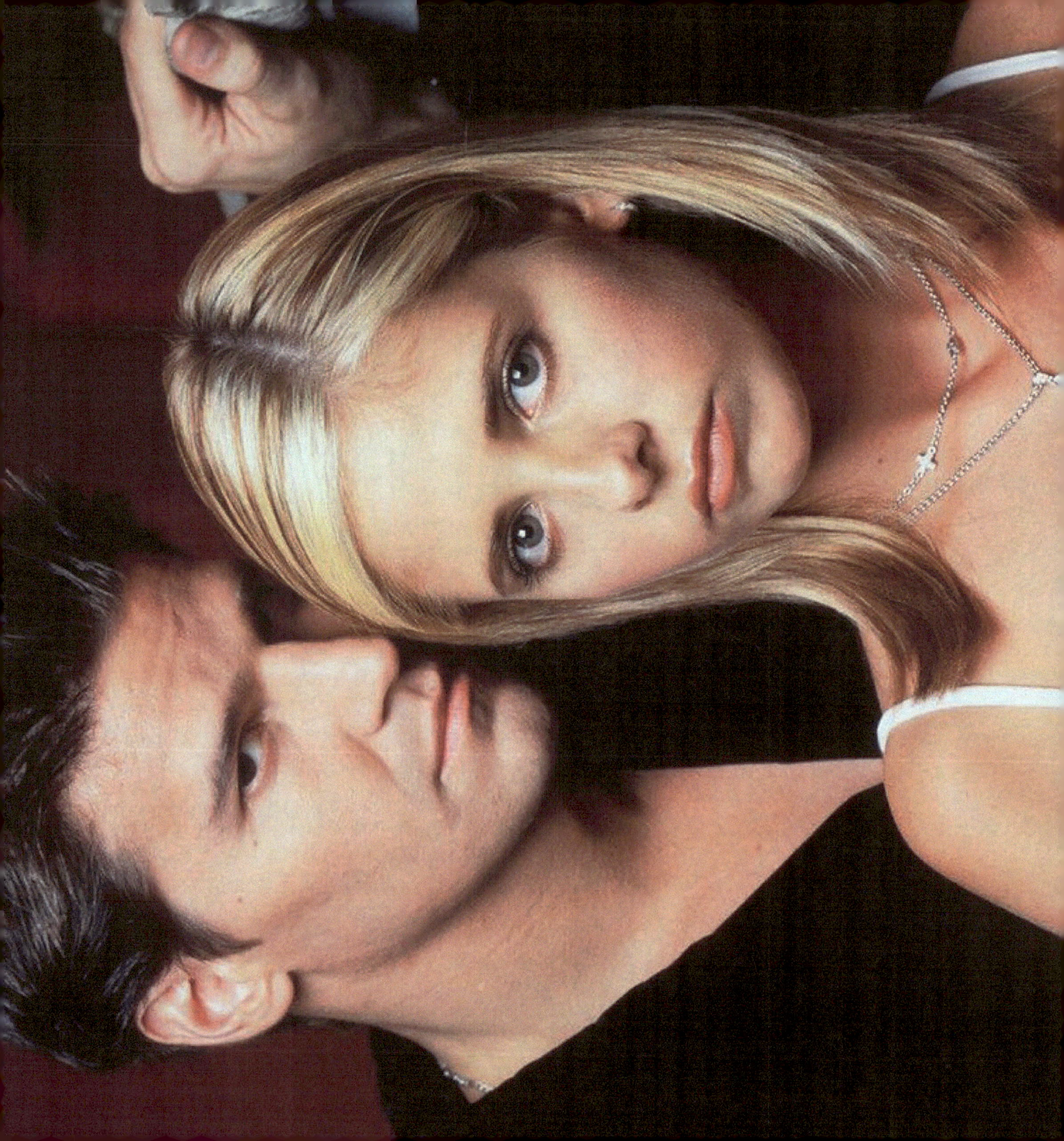

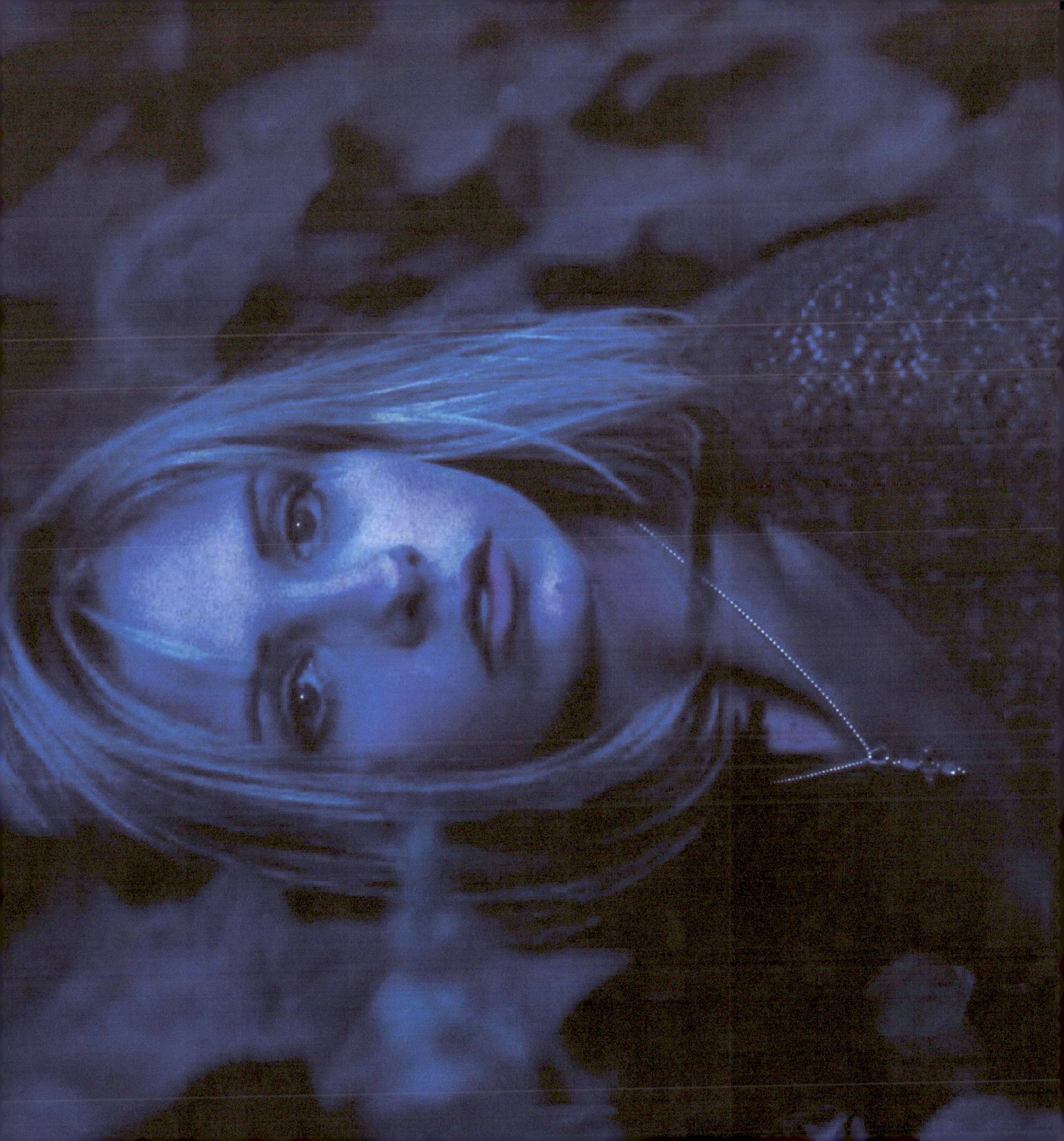

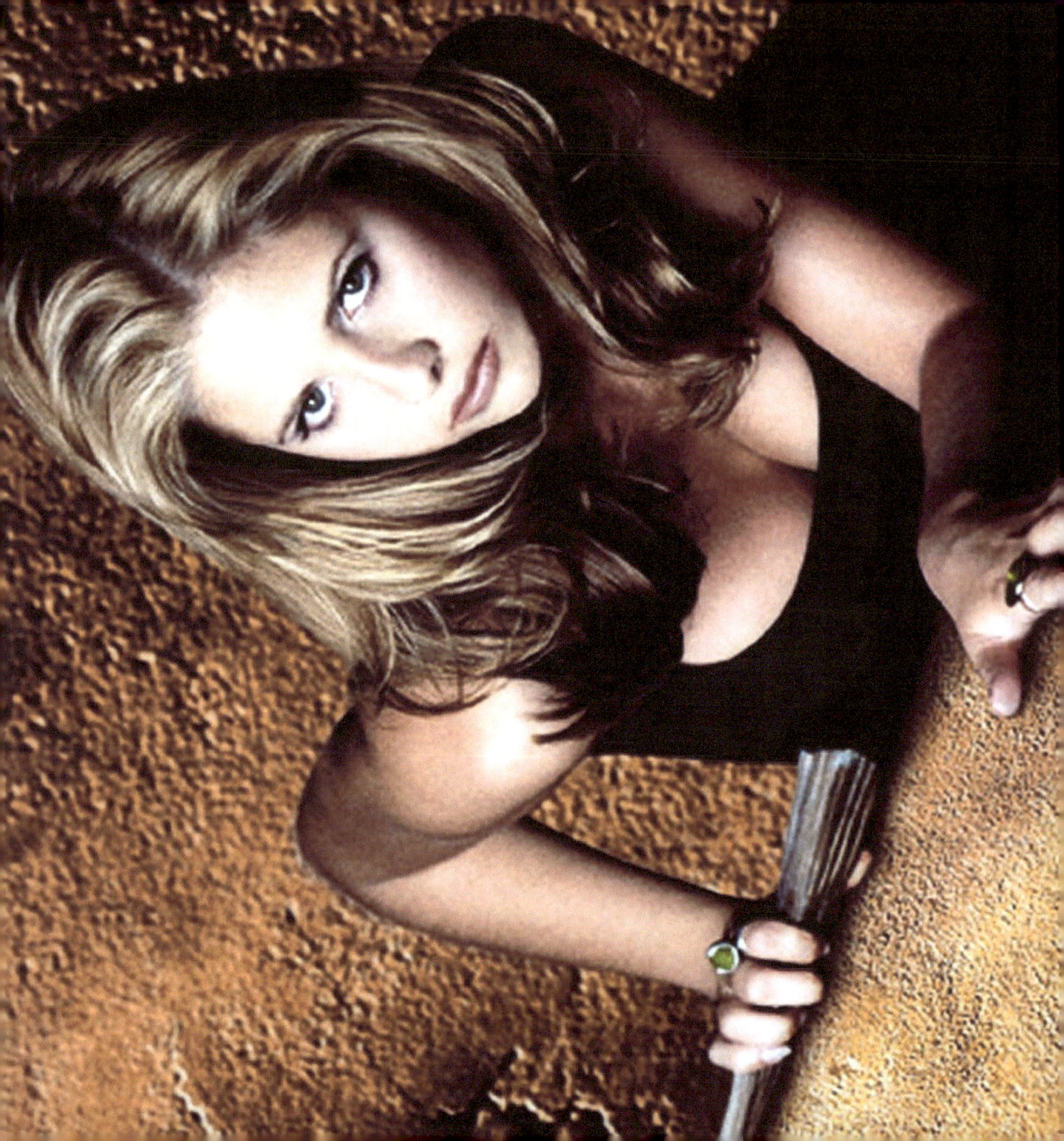

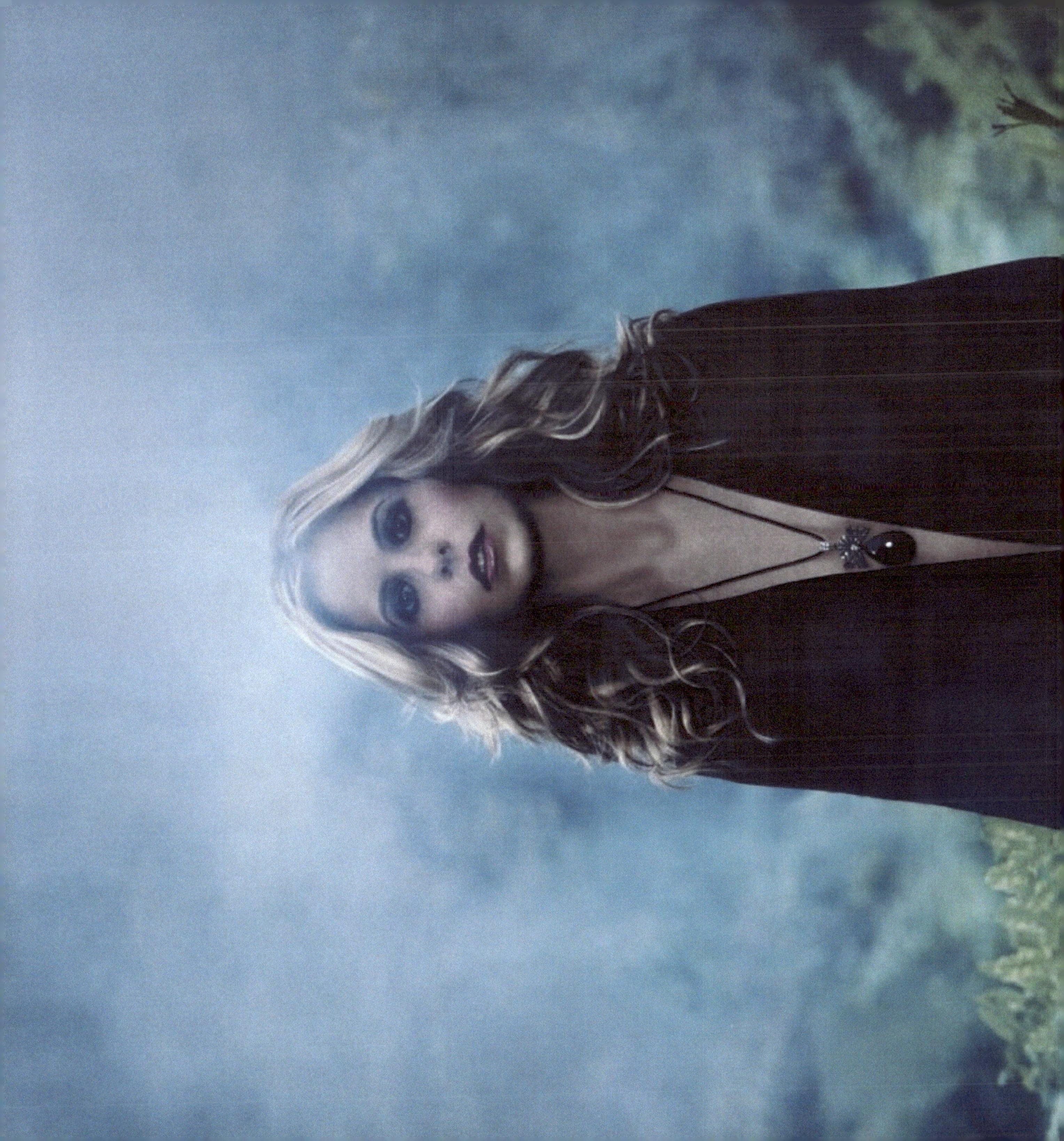

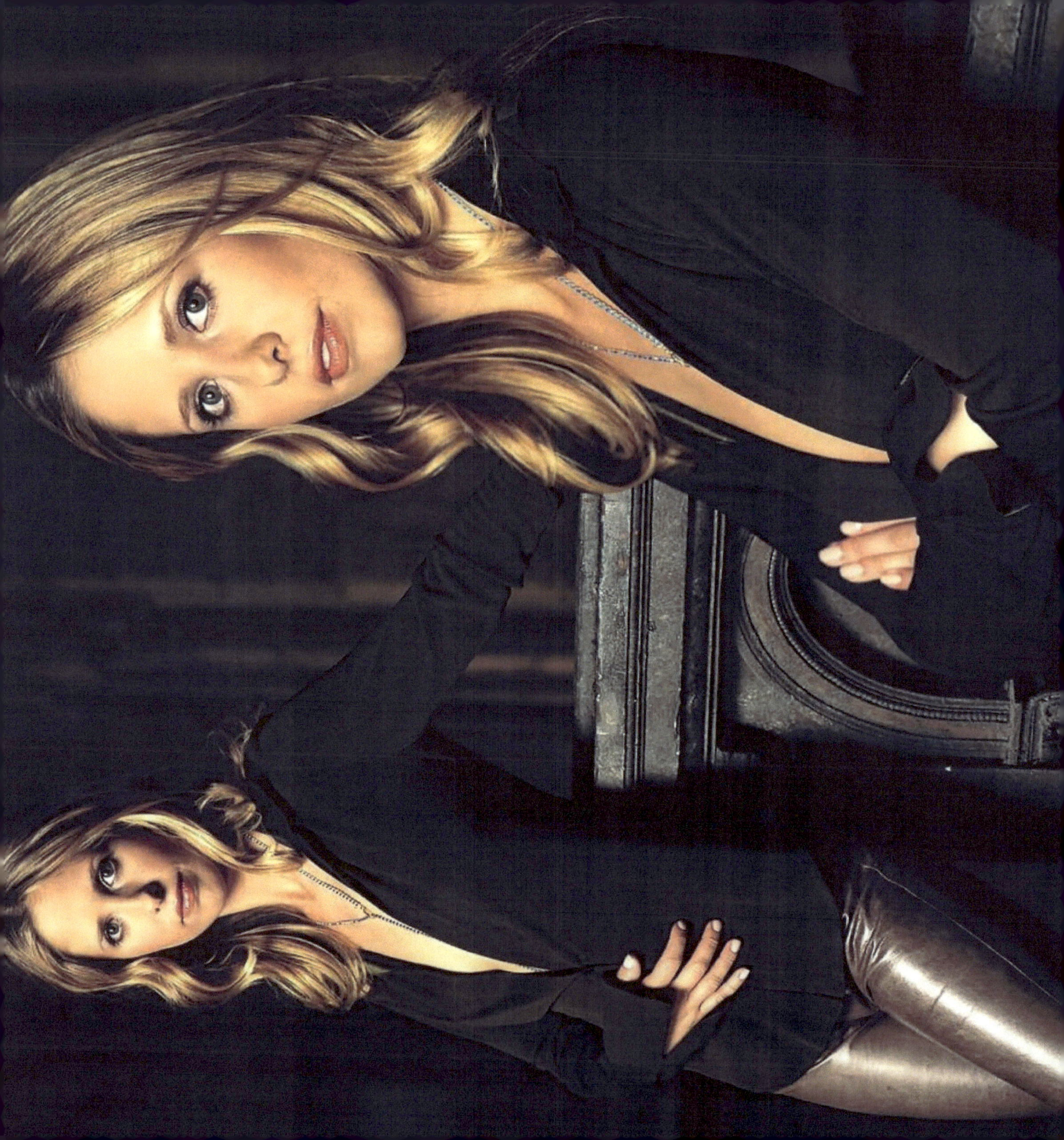

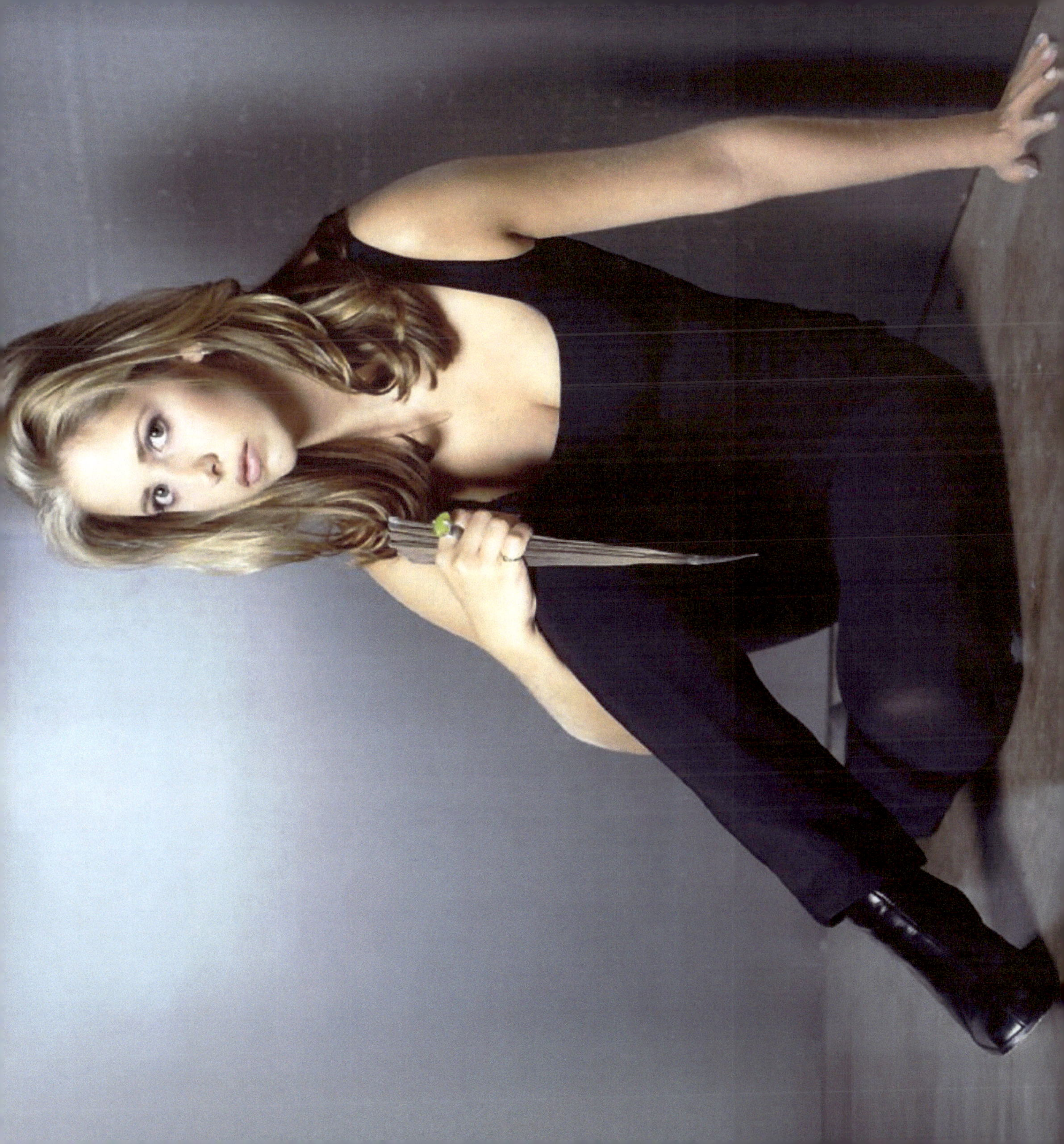

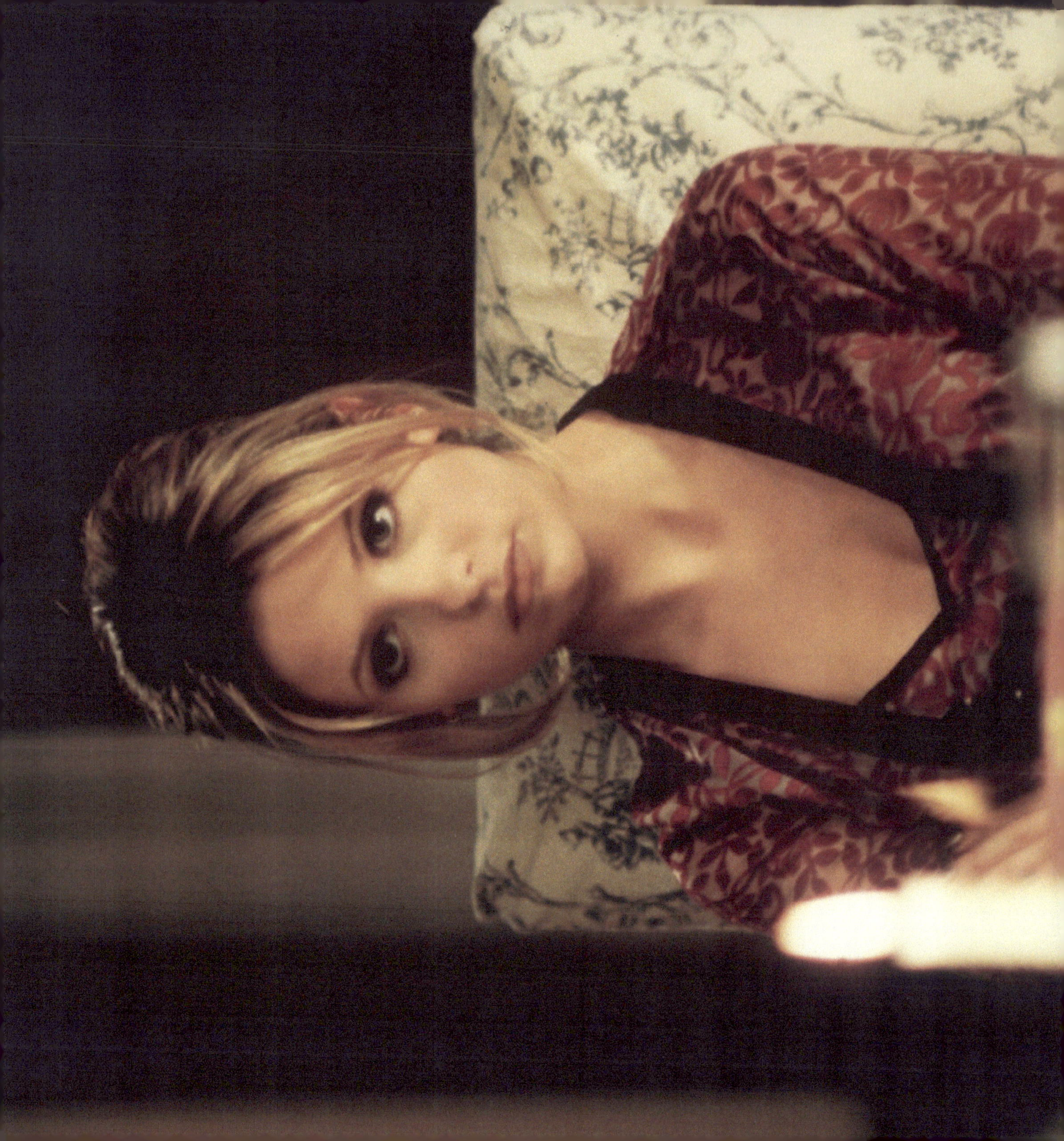